SNAP!

Written by
Marcia Vaughan

Illustrated by
Sascha Hutchinson

SCHOLASTIC
HARDCOVER

SCHOLASTIC INC.

New York

For Sam,
whose love of playing games
inspired this story
— M.V.

For Melinda, Kerrie,
and Margie
— S.H.

Text copyright © 1994 by Marcia Vaughan
Illustrations copyright © 1994 by Sascha Hutchinson
All rights reserved. Published by Scholastic Inc., 555 Broadway, New York, NY 10012
by arrangement with Omnibus Books.

Library of Congress Cataloging-in-Publication Data
Vaughan, Marcia K.
Snap! / by Marcia Vaughan; illustrated by Sascha Hutchinson.
p.   cm.
Summary: Joey the kangaroo plays games with Twisker the bush
mouse, Slider the snake, Prickler the echidna, Flatso the platypus,
and Sly-tooth the crocodile.
ISBN 0-590-60377-9
[1. Kangaroos—Fiction. 2. Animals—Fiction. 3. Zoology—
Australia—Fiction. 4. Australia—Fiction. 5. Games—Fiction.]
I. Hutchinson, Sascha, ill. II. Title.
PZ7.V452Sn 1996
[E]—dc20   95-11773
CIP
AC

12 11 10 9 8 7 6 5 4 3 2 1   6 7 8 9/9 0 1/0

Printed in Singapore
First printing, May 1996
The illustrations in this book
are torn paper collages.

It was a sun-hot, sky-dry day as Joey and Mama Roo stopped to drink at the edge of the Tumba-Rumba River.

"Mother, Mother, what do you say?" said Joey. "Do you know any games to play? I've been sitting in this pouch *all* day."

His mother yawned. "It's much too hot to play today."

Mama Roo settled in the shade and shut her eyes. She soon began to snore. *Wheesh-hoosh, wheesh-hoosh.*

Joey was not sleepy. Not one bit.
Peeking over the edge of his mother's
pouch, he saw a bush mouse pattering past.
"Twisker, Twisker, what do you say? Do you
know any games to play?" called Joey.

"I do," twittered Twisker. "I know a great game. But it's too hot to teach you today."

"Please stay. Don't go away," said Joey. "We can play together *all* day."

So Twisker tiptoed into the shade of the river rocks and taught Joey how to play hide-and-squeak.

Peeking around the rocks, Joey saw a snake slowly slithering by.

"Slider, Slider, what do you say? Do you know any games to play?"

"Yes, yess, yessss," hissed Slider. "I know a sssplendid game. But it'sss too hot to teach you today."

"Please stay. Don't go away. We can play together *all* day."

So Slider slid through the tall grass and taught the two to play lots-of-knots.

Peeking through the grass, Joey saw a platypus paddling past.

"Flatso, Flatso, what do you say? Do you know any games to play?"

"Of course I do," huffed Flatso. "I know a gooey game. But it's too hot to teach you today."

"Please stay. Don't go away. We can play together *all* day."

So Flatso flopped out of the water and taught the three to play pass-the-mudpie.

Peeking along the bank, Joey saw an echidna burrowing out of a termite mound.

"Prickler, Prickler, what do you say? Do you know any games to play?"

"Indeed I do," declared Prickler. "I know a nifty game. But it's too hot to teach you today."

"Please stay. Don't go away. We can play together *all* day."

So Prickler waddled into a hollow log and
taught the four to play pick-up-quills.

Peeking out of the log, Joey saw a
long, strong crocodile creeping up
the bank of the Tumba-Rumba River.

"Sly-tooth, Sly-tooth, what do you say?
Do you know any games to play?"

"Certainly I do," said Sly-tooth with a
wicked grin. "I know the best game in the
whole wide world. But it's too hot to teach
you today."

"Please stay. Don't go away," cried Joey.
"We can play together *all* day."

Just then Sly-tooth spied Joey's four friends.
"I'll stay for a moment then," he agreed.
"My game does not take long to play. Come
closer and do as I say. When I open my
magnificent jaws, you must all hurry inside.
I will hide you so well that nobody could
ever find you.

"Can you guess the name of my wonderful game?" asked Sly-tooth.

He stretched his jaw as wide as a cave.

"Hide-and-squeak?" asked Twisker.
"Lots-of-knots?" hissed Slider.
"Pass-the-mudpie?" said Flatso.

"Pick-up-quills?" guessed Prickler.
"We don't know," said Joey. "What is the name
of this wonderful game?"

Sly-tooth took a great, deep breath and went

SNAP!

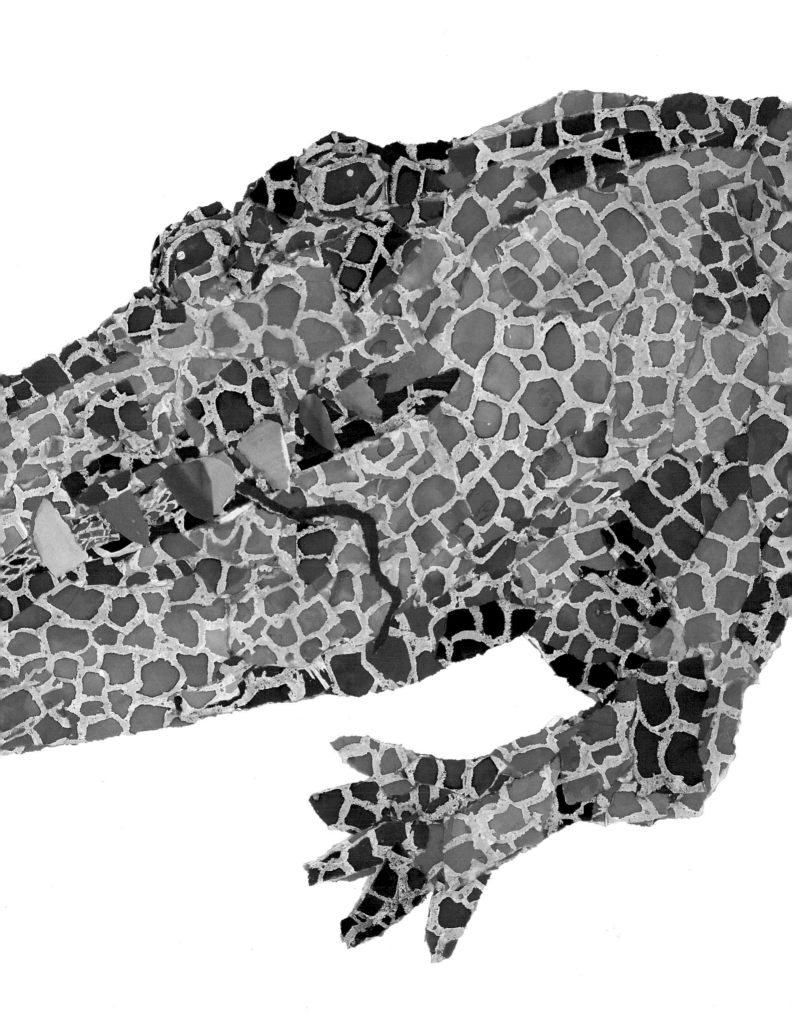

"We're trapped!" squeaked Twisker.
"There's no way out," sniffled Slider.
"We're goners," groaned Flatso.
"It's hopeless," whimpered Prickler.

But Joey said, "Listen, my friends, what do you say? I know one last game to play."

"A game," gasped the animals. "Now?"

"Yes," nodded Joey. "I know the funniest game in the whole wide world. It's called tickle-the-tonsils."

Suddenly, deep down inside, Sly-tooth felt

a wiggling-jiggling,

twittering-jittering,

rollicking-frollicking,

reeling-feeling zinging up and down and
all around his bumpy body.

"Er-her," Sly-tooth grinned.
"Hardy-ho-hum," he wiggled,
squeezing his jaws together tightly.

Joey and his friends tickled those tonsils
and tickled those tonsils until a smile

split Sly-tooth's jaws wide open and out
burst an earth-quaking, sky-shaking

WHOA HO HEE HAR HOOEY HOO HOOOOOO!

Twisker, Slider, Flatso, Prickler, and Joey sailed high into the air.

Sly-tooth was laughing so hard he could not stop. He whooped and howled and snortled and yowled all the way down the bank into the Tumba-Rumba River and floated far, far away.

Just then, Mama Roo opened her eyes. "Joey, my darling, what do you say? Do you know a game? I'm ready to play!"

But Joey did not answer. He jumped deep down to the very bottom of Mama Roo's pouch and wouldn't come out for a long, long time.

ANIMAL GLOSSARY

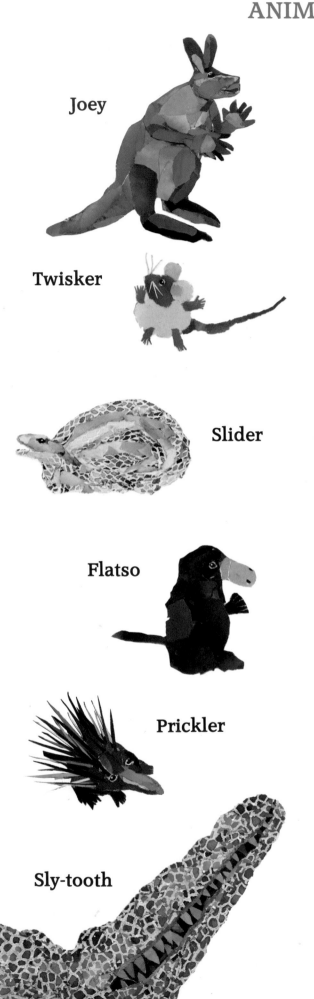

Joey

species: **Kangaroo**
animal class: **mammal**
favorite food: **grass**
special feature: **A kangaroo's powerful back legs
help it jump very fast.**

Twisker

species: **Hopping-mouse (also called bush mouse)**
animal class: **mammal**
favorite food: **seeds, plants, insects**
special feature: **A hopping-mouse's big ears and long
tail make it easy to recognize.**

Slider

species: **Green Tree Snake**
animal class: **reptile**
favorite food: **frogs and small lizards**
special feature: **A green tree snake's quickness
helps it capture food.**

Flatso

species: **Platypus**
animal class: **mammal**
favorite food: **shellfish and worms**
special feature: **A platypus's webbed feet help it move
easily in the water.**

Prickler

species: **Echidna**
animal class: **mammal**
favorite food: **termites and ants**
special feature: **An echidna uses its long, sharp quills
to protect itself from enemies.**

Sly-tooth

species: **Crocodile**
animal class: **reptile**
favorite food: **fish and small animals**
special feature: **A crocodile can weigh
up to 1,300 pounds.**